Tractor Mac

ARRIVES AT THE FARM

written and illustrated by Billy Steers

This book is for Julie.
Love, Billy

Sibley the Horse lived on Stony Meadow Farm. He was a hard worker. Tug and pull, haul and drag. He did the work of two strong horses.

Sibley's days were spent plowing in the spring, mowing in the summer,

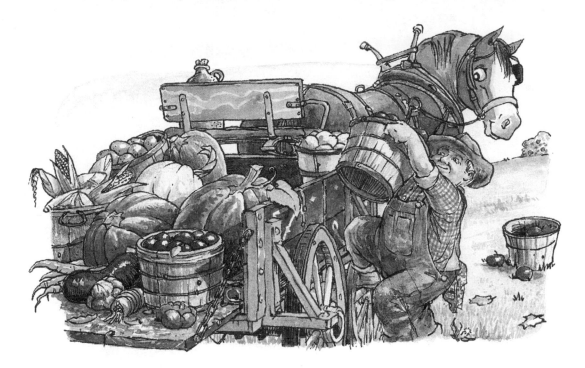

harvesting in the fall, and logging in the winter.

Sibley's favorite job was pulling the hayride at the summer picnics.

The children would all cheer for Sibley and give him treats of apples and carrots.

One day, the animals heard a strange, new noise in the farmyard. *Chug! Chugga! Pop!*

They looked out of the barn.

A large red machine sat in the farmyard spewing smoke. Farmer Bill was seated on a bright, new, shiny tractor. He had a big smile on his face.

That evening
Farmer Bill parked
the tractor in the barn.
The animals came over
to greet the newcomer.

"What big, black,
rubber tires you have,"
said Carla the Chicken.

"Look at all of your wires, gears, and cables!" exclaimed Pete the Pig.

"Welcome to Stony Meadow Farm," greeted Sam the Old Ram.

"Welcome!
Welcome!" the
others cried.

The red tractor smiled. "Howdy Do!" he said. "My name is Mac. I can do the work of ten horses, and I'm happy to be here."

"Ten horses!" gasped the animals. "You must be *really* strong."

That night, Sibley was not able to sleep. Visions of mechanical horses danced in his head. Could Mac really do the work of ten horses? What would be left for Sibley to do?

Early the next morning, Farmer Bill climbed into Mac's seat and started the engine. Mac rumbled to life, and they headed for the fields. Sibley waited to be tacked up for the day's work, but nobody came.

All that day, Sibley listened to the other animals.

"Did you see how fast Mac plowed the fields?" cackled the chickens.

"He delivered the hay in less than an hour," the sheep exclaimed.

"He hauled all the wood for the new roof," squealed the pigs.

As the days passed, it was clear that Mac had taken over all of Sibley's jobs.

"Soon they'll be turning you out to pasture," said Margot the Cow. "You'll probably never have to work another day in your life."

Just then, Sibley heard the sound of children.

Maybe they were coming to the

barnyard for a hayride.

He galloped out

of the barn....

…and stopped abruptly at the fence. There was Mac, pulling a dozen cheering children in a hay wagon. Sibley's hay wagon!

Sibley had never felt so sad and useless in his whole life. What good is a workhorse who cannot work?

In the weeks that followed, Sibley
hoped he would be put to work. But
every morning, Farmer Bill and Mac
left the barn. Sibley wondered if he
had been forgotten for good.

Finally, one day Farmer Bill came back to the farm without Mac. "Sibley, old lad, I need your help. We have a problem that only you can fix." The farmer led Sibley to one of the far fields. Rain had fallen during the night. The field was soaked with rainwater. There sat Mac up to his axles in mud.

With a tug and a yank, Sibley wrenched Mac free from the mud.

Then he spent the rest of the day working in the soggy field while Mac sat behind the stone wall.

When it was time to go back to the barn, Mac said, "Thanks for rescuing me, Sibley."

Farmer Bill patted Sibley on the neck. "You were a big help today," he said.

From that day on, Farmer Bill let
both Sibley and Mac work side by side.
They became the best of friends.